P9-CCH-052

A VERY
SPECIAL HOUSE

BY RUTH KRAUSS

PICTURES BY MAURICE SENDAK

HARPER & ROW, PUBLISHERS, NEW YORK, EVANSTON, AND LONDON

BOOKS BY RUTH KRAUSS

 The Carrot Seed

The Growing Story

 Bears

The Happy Day

 The Backward Day

The Bundle Book

 A Hole Is To Dig

A Very Special House

dee dee dee oh-h-h

I know a house—
it's not a squirrel house
it's not a donkey house
—it's not a house you'd see—
and it's not in any street
and it's not in any road—
oh it's just a house for me Me ME.

There's a bed that's very special
and a shelf that's very special
and the chairs are very special
—but it's not to take a seat—
and the doors are very special
and the walls are very special and
a table very special where to put your feet feet feet.

SPECIAL

SPECIAL

I'm bringing home a turtle
and a rabbit and a giant
and a little dead mouse
—I take it everywheres—
and some monkeys and some skunkeys
and a very old lion which . . .

MOUSE

. . . is eating all the stuffings from the chairs chairs chairs.

They and I are making secrets
and we're falling over laughing
and we're running in and out
—and we hooie hooie hooie—
then we think we are some chickens
then we're singing in the opera then
we're going going going going ooie ooie ooie.

WHOOP! WHOOP! WHOOP!
SOMETHING'S IN THE SOUP

OOIE

HE
HA.

Oh ooie ooie ooie ooie
ooie ooie ooie—we're
sprinkling cracker crumbs under all the cushions and
that lion's keeping snoring—going snore snore snore—and
the monkeys are all dancing with a special monkey-feeling
—like they're leaving little feetprints on the ceiling
ceiling ceiling—and I'm hopping and I'm skipping and I'm
jumping and I'm bumping—and Everywhere is music—and
the giant spilled his drinking and it went all down the floor
and the rabbit ate a piece out of my very best door
and Everybody's yelling for more More MORE.

MORE MORE MORE
MORE MORE MORE
MORE MORE MORE MORE
—blop blop blop—
MORE MORE MORE MORE
MORE MORE MORE MORE
NOBODY ever says stop stop stop.

I know a house—
it's not a squirrel house
it's not a donkey house
—just like I said—
and it's not up on a mountain
and it's not down in a valley
and it's not down in a hole
and it's not down in our alley
and it's not up in a tree
or underneath the bed—
oh it's right in the middle—
oh it's ret in the meedle—
oh it's root in the moodle of my head head head.

dee dee dee oh
doh doh doh-h-h-h